The Busy Tree

by

Jennifer Ward

illustrated by

Lisa Falkenstern

two lions

I'm a tree, a busy tree . . .
come and see.

These are my roots, winding and long;
they anchor and feed me and help me grow strong.

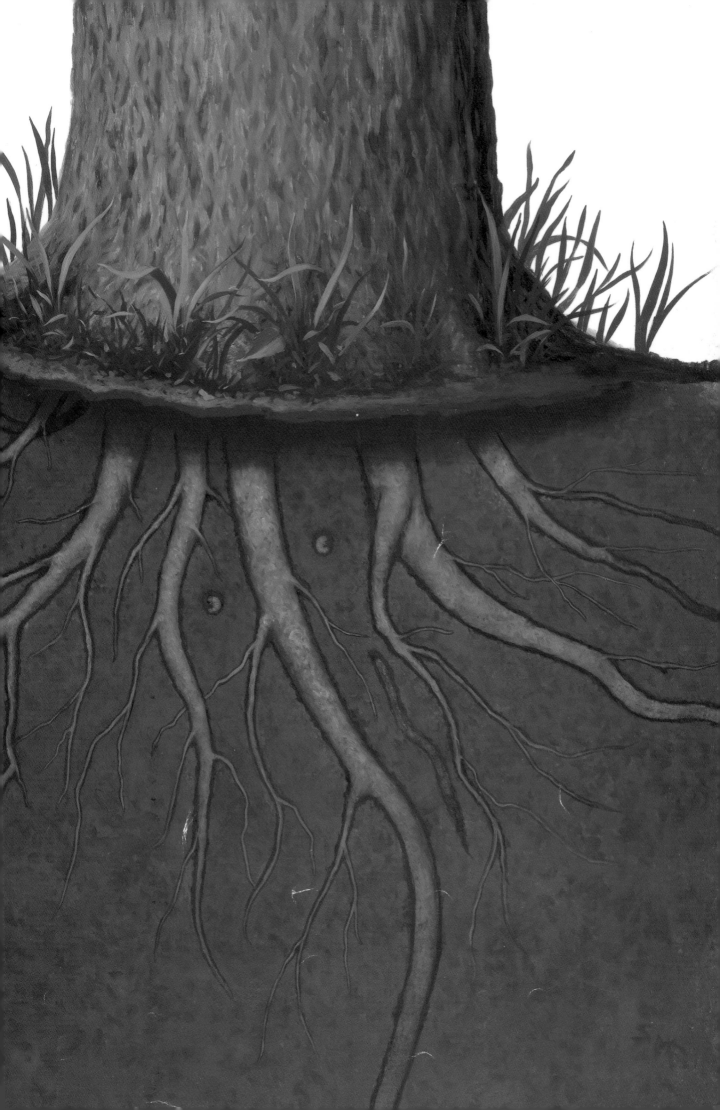

Look at my acorns, shiny and round,
nibbled by chipmunks who scratch at the ground.

Here is my trunk, where busy ants scurry,
searching for food as they march in a hurry.

This is the spider that lives in my bark,
spinning a web from dawn until dark.

A woodpecker searches, eager to munch,
tapping for bugs it will eat for its lunch.

Visit my hollow that is home to an owl;

he sleeps all day long, then at night starts to prowl.

These are my branches, leafy and high,
a sidewalk for squirrels that soar through the sky.

One of my branches cradles a nest,
a cozy, warm home where new hatchlings rest.

Look at this small twig that holds a cocoon,
protecting a moth that will emerge soon.

Hear my green leaves as they shake in the wind,
breathing out air for all to breathe in.

These are my boughs that creak, bend, and sway,
shading the children below as they play.

A boy finds an acorn I shake from my top
among autumn leaves that swirl as they drop.

A girl plants a seed,

it grows toward the sky,

taller and stronger as seasons pass by,

becoming a tree, a busy tree . . . .

Come and see!

To my sisters, Cathy, Laura, Kristen, and Debbie
—J.W.
To my husband, Ken, who changed my life
—L.F.

two lions

Text copyright © 2009 by Jennifer Ward
Illustrations copyright © 2009 by Lisa Falkenstern

Amazon Publishing
Attn: Amazon Children's Publishing, P.O. Box 400818, Las Vegas, NV 89140
www.marshallcavendish.us/kids

Library of Congress Cataloging-in-Publication Data
Ward, Jennifer.
The busy tree / by Jennifer Ward ; illustrated by Lisa Falkenstern. — 1st ed.
    p. cm.
Summary: Many different types of wildlife live in and around a tree that is
their home, from chipmunks and woodpeckers to ants and spiders.
ISBN 978-0-7614-5550-9
[1. Stories in rhyme. 2. Trees—Fiction. 3. Forest animals—Fiction.]
I. Falkenstern, Lisa, ill. II. Title.
PZ8.3.W2135Bu 2009
[E]—dc22
2008006005

The illustrations were rendered in oil paint.
Book design by Vera Soki
Editor: Margery Cuyler

Printed in China
First edition
564